I AM
THE DARKER
BROTHER

I AM
THE DARKER
BROTHER

AN ANTHOLOGY OF MODERN POEMS
BY BLACK AMERICANS

EDITED BY *Arnold Adoff*

DRAWINGS BY *Benny Andrews*

FOREWORD BY *Charlemae Rollins*

COLLIER BOOKS
Division of Macmillan Publishing Co., Inc.
New York

Macmillan Publishing Co., Inc.
866 Third Avenue, New York, N.Y. 10022
Collier Macmillan Canada, Inc.

Library of Congress catalog card number: 68-12077
I Am the Darker Brother is published in a
hardcover edition by Macmillan Publishing Co., Inc.

Printed in the United States of America

FIRST COLLIER BOOKS EDITION 1970
14   13   12   11   10   9   8   7

ACKNOWLEDGMENTS

Thanks are due to the following for permission to include copy-
righted selections:

Samuel Allen (Paul Vesey) for his "If the Stars Should Fall," "A
Moment Please" and "American Gothic."

Arna Bontemps for his "A Black Man Talks of Reaping," "Southern
Mansion" and "The Daybreakers" from *American Negro Poetry*
(Hill & Wang), edited by Arna Bontemps.

Harper & Row, Publishers, for "Bronzeville Man with a Belt in the
Back," Copyright © 1960 by Gwendolyn Brooks Blakely; "We Real
Cool," Copyright © 1959 by Gwendolyn Brooks Blakely and "A
Song in the Front Yard," Copyright 1945 by Gwendolyn Brooks
Blakely; from *Selected Poems* by Gwendolyn Brooks.

Sterling A. Brown for his "Old Lem."

Harper & Row, Publishers, for "Incident"; "For a Lady I
Know"; "Yet Do I Marvel," Copyright 1925 by Harper &
Brothers, renewed 1953 by Ida M. Cullen and "From the
Dark Tower," Copyright 1927 by Harper & Brothers, re-

for Jaime Levi Adoff,
in memory of Langston Hughes

Contents

SHALL BE REMEMBERED

IF WE MUST DIE

I AM THE DARKER BROTHER

THE HOPE OF YOUR UNBORN

Foreword

Should you stand at the edge of a South Side playground in Chicago and listen to the children at their games, you would hear their palms clapping, their voices lifted in a singsong chant, and see their hips and arms and bodies swaying in rhythms unlike those of any other American children. It is not one song, but a dozen, with patterns of words unheard elsewhere, about corn bread, and stepping out to the dance, and Saturday nights, and all the delights that are not wholly denied them.

Of this great mass of dark-skinned children it has been said that they are culturally deprived, yet here is a culture as spontaneous as it is unrecognized. It tells us again that the spirit of man can still endure under whatever misery and deprivation, on crowded streets and in back alleys where the garbage cans overflow, that here there is even laughter and dance and song.

It is out of this background that most present day Negro poets have come—the urban ghettoes of our great cities, North and South. An earlier day was more rural, and some of its poets delighted in bright sun and warm rain, the winds and soil and growing things. Today few such poets appear. The city is the environment which brings the greatest pressure and produces the greatest literature in our time.

Among the many who have written distinguished poetry in the twentieth century, and who are represented in this anthology, perhaps the best known are Langston Hughes, Margaret Walker, and Gwendolyn Brooks, and only less frequently mentioned are

Countee Cullen and Claude McKay. More recently we have Mari Evans, with her delightful humor and penetrating insights, and Conrad Kent Rivers, who finds poetry in the city scene. These younger poets still have many years of creativity before them and their fame will not rest only on the poems included here.

It seemed to me a great honor to be asked to write an introduction for so discriminating an anthology as this assembled by Arnold Adoff. I am only a librarian —and a children's librarian at that—not a *littérateur*. But then, perhaps, it is only natural that a librarian should be invited to comment on this poetry. Langston Hughes, in his loneliness and bitterness, found himself in the Cleveland Public Library one day, and there Effie Power, a truly great and far-seeing librarian, became his friend.

She introduced him to books—great books, literature and poetry—and so, even in his teens, he began writing voluminously. She often pinned his poems on the bulletin board in the library, giving him his first "publication" and his first, and most necessary, encouragement. He tells with warmth of this encounter in his autobiographical writings, and says that to Miss Power he was neither white nor black, but simply a poet and a writer.

Another children's librarian, Marian Hadley, loomed large in the life of Gwendolyn Brooks, our only Negro poet to have won the Pulitzer Prize for poetry. Here in Chicago, Miss Hadley, at the small South Side Sub Branch, supplied the young Gwendolyn with all the books so necessary for her development and growth. Gwendolyn Brooks, quite different in background from Langston Hughes in spite of her urban environment, was protected and gently reared in a comfortable home. She grew up without bitterness, but it was from her observation of the children of poverty all about her that she drew her most telling vignettes in "A Street in Bronzeville," and found the materials for her distinguished career.

Perhaps some librarian—or teacher or parent—will find in this small volume material to illuminate and inspire another generation of poets and writers. Poetry is not easy for many people, young or old, to read. Most of our lives we spend reading and studying prose, and especially is this true in our high school and college years, when textbooks are our heaviest fare—and textbooks are not poetry!

Prose can expand and explain, but poetry must be felt. It is through feeling that the reader finds the meanings and emotions the poet has expressed in concise, compressed, symbolic, and figurative language. From such literature, as the Greeks discovered long ago, we find catharsis—the ridding ourselves of the emotions of hate and envy, and even of the will to murder and destroy.

In this way our greatest poets become our greatest educators, illuminating our past, shining light into our future, but most of all, helping us to recognize what is most tragic as well as most hopeful in our present. This is why, at times, some recent poems shock us with their outspoken language. Yet poets of today must use the language of today if they are to reach the deepest emotions of their contemporaries.

As a librarian, and a hopeful guide to young people whatever the color of their skin, I often think of Effie Power who long ago made Langston Hughes feel that he was neither black nor white, that he was just a writer with an immense need for books all around him.

A touching story, recounted by Claude Brown in his *Manchild in the Promised Land*, tells of Eleanor Roosevelt, and how she gave him a book while he was still in Wiltwyck, the reform school for boys. This, he says, opened the world of books to him and so changed his whole life. Perhaps some young person, browsing through this anthology, will come upon a poem or many poems that will lead him to other books and other poets and into the whole range of English literature—and thus another poet and writer may be born.

Chicago, Illinois   CHARLEMAE ROLLINS
1968

Preface

This anthology was created to present good, interesting, and evocative poems by Negro Americans; poems to be enjoyed and remembered, poems outstanding in their ethnic vision.

I felt there was a great need at this time to make these poems easily available to both Negroes and whites. The poems stand as statements that should live in print because their authors have put a part of life into music and language. Robert Hayden has defined poetry as "The beauty of perception given form . . . the art of saying the impossible." A poet writes from the need to create beauty. A poet who is black writes from a special knowledge of life in this country.

There is a need for Negroes to know of and experience through the eyes of other Negroes how it has been and how it is to be a Negro in America, and for whites to become familiar with this part of their American heritage through the vision of life as Negroes in this country see it.

I have been a teacher in New York City for almost ten years, and have come to know the anthologies of American poetry used in the schools, with their nearly total lack of inclusion of Negro American poets, with the occasional exception of a Hughes, Brooks, or Cullen poem.

It is hoped that this anthology will help to make Negro American poets more visible, and that the reader will continue from this book to the published works of the authors represented here, as well as to those other poets whose work could not be included because of limitations of space.

With more than twenty-two million of America's citizens now struggling for true equality in all areas of American life, poems by Negroes may someday receive the recognition in anthologies which has previously been denied them. Until this time of artistic integration, however, volumes such as this one will be necessary to present a nation's great literary heritage to its people.

New York City
1968

ARNOLD ADOFF

LIKE I AM

Me and the Mule

LANGSTON HUGHES

My old mule,
He's got a grin on his face.
He's been a mule so long
He's forgot about his race.

I'm like that old mule—
Black—and don't give a damn!
You got to take me
Like I am.

The Rebel

Mari Evans

When I
die
I'm sure
I will have a
Big Funeral ...
Curiosity
seekers ...
coming to see
if I
am really
Dead ...
or just
trying to make
Trouble ....

We Real Cool

GWENDOLYN BROOKS

The Pool Players
Seven At the Golden Shovel

We real cool. We
Left school. We

Lurk late. We
Strike straight. We

Sing sin. We
Thin gin. We

Jazz June. We
Die soon.

Cross

LANGSTON HUGHES

My old man's a white old man
And my old mother's black.
If ever I cursed my white old man
I take my curses back.

If ever I cursed my black old mother
And wished she were in hell,
I'm sorry for that evil wish
And now I wish her well.

My old man died in a fine big house.
My ma died in a shack.
I wonder where I'm gonna die,
Being neither white nor black?

Aunt Jane Allen

FENTON JOHNSON

State Street is lonely today. Aunt Jane Allen has
  driven her chariot to Heaven.
I remember how she hobbled along, a little woman,
  parched of skin, brown as the leather of a satchel
  and with eyes that scanned eighty years of life.
Have those who bore her dust to the last resting place
  buried with her the basket of aprons she went up
  and down State Street trying to sell?
Have those who bore her dust to the last resting place
  buried with her the gentle word *Son* that she gave
  to each of the seed of Ethiopia?

The Whipping

ROBERT HAYDEN

The old woman across the way
   is whipping the boy again
and shouting to the neighborhood
   her goodness and his wrongs.

Wildly he crashes through elephant ears,
   pleads in dusty zinnias,
while she in spite of crippling fat
   pursues and corners him.

She strikes and strikes the shrilly circling
   boy till the stick breaks
in her hand. His tears are rainy weather
   to woundlike memories:

My head gripped in bony vise
   of knees, the writhing struggle
to wrench free, the blows, the fear
   worse than blows that hateful

Words could bring, the face that I
   no longer knew or loved . . .
Well, it is over now, it is over,
   and the boy sobs in his room,

And the woman leans muttering against
   a tree, exhausted, purged—
avenged in part for lifelong hidings
   she has had to bear.

Those
Winter Sundays

ROBERT HAYDEN

Sundays too my father got up early
and put his clothes on in the blueblack cold,
then with cracked hands that ached
from labor in the weekday weather made
banked fires blaze. No one ever thanked him.

I'd wake and hear the cold splintering, breaking.
When the rooms were warm, he'd call,
and slowly I would rise and dress,
fearing the chronic angers of that house,

Speaking indifferently to him,
who had driven out the cold
and polished my good shoes as well.
What did I know, what did I know
of love's austere and lonely offices?

A Song in the Front Yard

GWENDOLYN BROOKS

I've stayed in the front yard all my life.
I want a peek at the back
Where it's rough and untended and hungry weed
   grows.
A girl gets sick of a rose.

I want to go in the back yard now
And maybe down the alley,
To where the charity children play.
I want a good time today.

They do some wonderful things.
They have some wonderful fun.
My mother sneers, but I say it's fine
How they don't have to go in at a quarter to nine.
My mother she tells me that Johnnie Mae
Will grow up to be a bad woman.
That George'll be taken to jail soon or late.
(On account of last winter he sold our back gate.)

But I say it's fine. Honest I do.
And I'd like to be a bad woman too,
And wear the brave stockings of night-black lace.
And strut down the streets with paint on my face.

Flowers
of Darkness

FRANK MARSHALL DAVIS

Slowly the night blooms, unfurling
Flowers of darkness, covering
The trellised sky, becoming
A bouquet of blackness
Unending
Touched with sprigs
Of pale and budding stars

Soft the night smell
Among April trees
Soft and richly rare
Yet commonplace
Perfume on a cosmic scale

I turn to you Mandy Lou
I see the flowering night
Cameo condensed
Into the lone black rose
Of your face
The young woman-smell
Of your poppy body
Rises to my brain as opium

Yet silently motionless
I sit with twitching fingers
Yea, even reverently

Sit I
With you and the blossoming night
For what flower, plucked,
Lingers long?

Juke Box
Love Song

LANGSTON HUGHES

I could take the Harlem night
and wrap around you,
Take the neon lights and make a crown,
Take the Lenox Avenue buses,
Taxis, subways,
And for your love song tone their rumble down.
Take Harlem's heartbeat,
Make a drumbeat,
Put it on a record, let it whirl,
And while we listen to it play,
Dance with you till day—
Dance with you, my sweet brown Harlem girl.

The Glory of the Day Was in Her Face

James Weldon Johnson

The glory of the day was in her face,
The beauty of the night was in her eyes.
And over all her loveliness, the grace
Of Morning blushing in the early skies.

And in her voice, the calling of the dove;
Like music of a sweet, melodious part.
And in her smile, the breaking light of love;
And all the gentle virtues in her heart.

And now the glorious day, the beauteous night,
The birds that signal to their mates at dawn,
To my dull ears, to my tear-blinded sight
Are one with all the dead, since she is gone.

Bronzeville Man
with a Belt
in the Back

GWENDOLYN BROOKS

In such an armor he may rise and raid
The dark cave after midnight, unafraid,
And slice the shadows with his able sword
Of good broad nonchalance, hashing them down.

And come out and accept the gasping crowd,
Shake off the praises with an airiness.
And, searching, see love shining in an eye,
But never smile.

In such an armor he cannot be slain.

Madhouse

CALVIN C. HERNTON

Here is a place that is no place
And here is no place that is a place
A place somewhere beyond the reaches of time
And beyond the reaches of those who in time
Bring flowers and fruit to this place,
Yet here is a definite place
And a definite time, fixed
In a timelessness of precise vantage
From which to view flowers and view fruit
And those who come bearing them.

Those who come by Sunday's habit are weary
And kiss us half-foreign but sympathetic,
Spread and eat noisily to crack the unbearable
Silence of this place:
They do not know that something must always come
From something and that nothing must come always
From nothing, and that nothing is always a thing

To drive us mad.

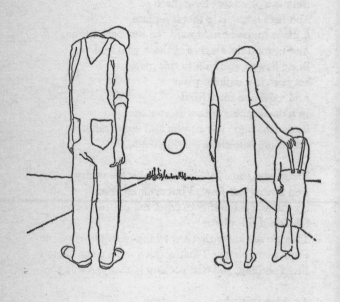

GENEALOGY

Each Morning

(Section 4 from
"Hymn For Lanie Poo")

LeRoi Jones

Each morning
I go down
to Gansevoort St.
and stand on the docks.
I stare out
at the horizon
until it gets up
and comes to embrace
me. I
make believe
it is my father.
This is known
as genealogy.

A Moment Please

SAMUEL ALLEN (PAUL VESEY)

When I gaze at the sun
   I walked to the subway booth
   for change for a dime.
and know that this great earth
   Two adolescent girls stood there
   alive with eagerness to know
is but a fragment from it thrown
   all in their new found world
   there was for them to know
in heat and flame a billion years ago,
   they looked at me and brightly asked
   "Are you Arabian?"
that then this world was lifeless
   I smiled and cautiously
   —for one grows cautious—
   shook my head.
as, a billion hence,
   "Egyptian?"
it shall again be,
   Again I smiled and shook my head
   and walked away.
what moment is it that I am betrayed,
   I've gone but seven paces now
oppressed, cast down,
   and from behind comes swift the sneer

or warm with love or triumph?
  "Or Nigger?"

  A moment, please
What is it that to fury I am roused?
  for still it takes a moment
What meaning for me
  and now
in this homeless clan
  I'll turn
the dupe of space
  and smile
the toy of time?
  and nod my head.

The Negro
Speaks of Rivers

To W. E. B. DuBois

Langston Hughes

I've known rivers:
I've known rivers ancient as the world and older than
the flow of human blood in human veins.

My soul has grown deep like the rivers.

I bathed in the Euphrates when dawns were young.
I built my hut near the Congo and it lulled me to
sleep.
I looked upon the Nile and raised the pyramids above
it.
I heard the singing of the Mississippi when Abe
Lincoln went down to New Orleans, and I've seen
its muddy bosom turn all golden in the sunset.
I've known rivers:
Ancient, dusky rivers.

My soul has grown deep like the rivers.

Southern Mansion

ARNA BONTEMPS

Poplars are standing there still as death
And ghosts of dead men
Meet their ladies walking
Two by two beneath the shade
And standing on the marble steps.

There is a sound of music echoing
Through the open door
And in the field there is
Another sound tinkling in the cotton:
Chains of bondmen dragging on the ground.

The years go back with an iron clank,
A hand is on the gate,
A dry leaf trembles on the wall.
Ghosts are walking.
They have broken roses down
And poplars stand there still as death.

O Daedalus,
Fly Away Home

ROBERT HAYDEN

Drifting night in the Georgia pines,
coonskin drum and jubilee banjo.
  Pretty Malinda, dance with me.

Night is juba, night is conjo.
  Pretty Malinda, dance with me.

Night is an African juju man
weaving a wish and a weariness together
  to make two wings.

  O fly away home fly away

Do you remember Africa?

  O cleave the air fly away home

My gran, he flew back to Africa,
just spread his arms and
  flew away home.

Drifting night in the windy pines;
night is a laughing, night is a longing.
  Pretty Malinda, come to me.

Night is a mourning juju man
weaving a wish and a weariness together
    to make two wings.

  O fly away home fly away

October Journey

Margaret Walker

Traveler take heed for journeys undertaken in the
    dark of the year.
Go in the bright blaze of Autumn's equinox.
Carry protection against ravages of a sun-robber, a
    vandal, and a thief.
Cross no bright expanse of water in the full of the
    moon.
Choose no dangerous summer nights;
no heady tempting hours of spring;
October journeys are safest, brightest, and best.

I want to tell you what hills are like in October
when colors gush down mountainsides
and little streams are freighted with a caravan of
    leaves.
I want to tell you how they blush and turn in fiery
    shame and joy,
how their love burns with flames consuming and
    terrible
until we wake one morning and woods are like a
    smoldering plain—
a glowing caldron full of jeweled fire:
the emerald earth a dragon's eye
the poplars drenched with yellow light
and dogwoods blazing bloody red.

Traveling southward earth changes from gray rock
   to green velvet.
Earth changes to red clay
with green grass growing brightly
with saffron skies of evening setting dully
with muddy rivers moving sluggishly.

In the early spring when the peach tree blooms
wearing a veil like a lavender haze
and the pear and plum in their bridal hair
gently snow their petals on earth's grassy bosom below
then the soughing breeze is soothing
and the world seems bathed in tenderness,
but in October
blossoms have long since fallen.
A few red apples hang on leafless boughs;
wind whips bushes briskly.
And where a blue stream sings cautiously
a barren land feeds hungrily.

An evil moon bleeds drops of death.
The earth burns brown.
Grass shrivels and dries to a yellowish mass.
Earth wears a dun-colored dress
like an old woman wooing the sun to be her lover,
be her sweetheart and her husband bound in one.
Farmers heap hay in stacks and bind corn in shocks
against the biting breath of frost.

The train wheels hum, "I am going home, I am going
   home,
I am moving toward the South."
Soon cypress swamps and muskrat marshes
and black fields touched with cotton will appear.

I dream again of my childhood land
of a neighbor's yard with a redbud tree
the smell of pine for turpentine
an Easter dress, a Christmas eve
and winding roads from the top of a hill.
A music sings within my flesh
I feel the pulse within my throat
my heart fills up with hungry fear
while hills and flatlands stark and staring
before my dark eyes sad and haunting
appear and disappear.

Then when I touch this land again
the promise of a sun-lit hour dies.
The greenness of an apple seems
to dry and rot before my eyes.
The sullen winter rains
are tears of grief I cannot shed.
The windless days are static lives.
The clock runs down
timeless and still.
The days and nights turn hours to years
and water in a gutter marks the circle of another
    world
hating, resentful, and afraid
stagnant, and green, and full of slimy things.

Dust Bowl

Robert A. Davis

These were our fields.
Now no flower blooms,
No grain grows here
Where earth moves in every wind.

No birds nest in these trees.
No fruit hangs
Where the boughs stretch bare
In the sun.

The dust sifts down—blows in.
Our mouths are filled.
The dust moves across,
And up and around the dust moves

In our waking—our sleeping—
In our dreams.

A Ballad
of Remembrance

ROBERT HAYDEN

Quadroon mermaids, Afro angels, black saints
balanced upon the switchblades of that air
and sang. Tight streets unfolding to the eye
like fans of corrosion and elegiac lace
crackled with their singing: Shadow of time. Shadow
  of blood.

Shadow, echoed the Zulu king, dangling
from a cluster of balloons. Blood,
whined the gun-metal priestess, floating
over the courtyard where dead men diced.

What will you have? she inquired, the sallow
  vendeuse
of prepared tarnishes and jokes of nacre and ormolu,
what but those gleamings, oldrose graces,
manners like scented gloves? Contrived ghosts
rapped to metronome clack of lavalieres.

Contrived illuminations riding a threat
of river, masked Negroes wearing chameleon
satins gaudy now as a fortuneteller's
dream of disaster, lighted the crazy flopping
dance of love and hate among joys, rejections.

Accommodate, muttered the Zulu king,
toad on a throne of glaucous poison jewels.
Love, chimed the saints and the angels and the
    mermaids.
Hate, shrieked the gun-metal priestess
from her spiked bellcollar curved like a fleur-de-lis:

As well have a talon as a finger, a muzzle as a mouth,
as well have a hollow as a heart. And she pinwheeled
away in coruscations of laughter, scattering
those others before her like foil stars.

But, the dance continued—now among metaphorical
doors, coffee cups floating poised
hysterias, decors of illusion; now among
mazurka dolls offering death's-heads
of cocaine roses and real violets.

Then you arrived, meditative, ironic,
richly human; and your presence was shore where I
    rested
released from the hoodoo of that dance, where I spoke
with my true voice again.

And therefore this is not only a ballad of remembrance
for the down-South arcane city with death
in its jaws like gold teeth and archaic cusswords;
not only a token for the troubled generous friends
held in the fists of that schizoid city like flowers,
but also, Mark Van Doren,
a poem of remembrance, a gift, a souvenir for you.

Middle Passage

ROBERT HAYDEN

I.

Jesús, Estrella, Esperanza, Mercy:

> Sails flashing to the wind like weapons,
> sharks following the moans the fever and the dying;
> horror the corposant and compass rose.

Middle Passage:
>   voyage through death
>   to life upon these shores.

> "10 April 1800—
> Blacks rebellious. Crew uneasy. Our linguist says
> their moaning is a prayer for death,
> ours and their own. Some try to starve themselves.
> Lost three this morning leaped with crazy laughter
> to the waiting sharks, sang as they went under."

Desire, Adventure, Tartar, Ann:

> Standing to America, bringing home
> black gold, black ivory, black seed.

Deep in the festering hold thy father lies,
of his bones New England pews are made,
those are altar lights that were his eyes.

Jesus Saviour Pilot Me
Over Life's Tempestuous Sea

We pray that Thou wilt grant, O Lord,
safe passage to our vessels bringing
heathen souls unto Thy chastening.

Jesus Saviour

"8 bells. I cannot sleep, for I am sick
with fear, but writing eases fear a little
since still my eyes can see these words take shape
upon the page & so I write, as one
would turn to exorcism. 4 days scudding,
but now the sea is calm again. Misfortune
follows in our wake like sharks (our grinning
tutelary gods). Which one of us
has killed an albatross? A plague among
our blacks—Ophthalmia: blindness—& we
have jettisoned the blind to no avail.
It spreads, the terrifying sickness spreads.
Its claws have scratched sight from the Capt.'s eyes
& there is blindness in the fo'c'sle
& we must sail 3 weeks before we come
to port."

> *What port awaits us, Davy Jones'*
> *or home? I've heard of slavers drifting, drifting,*
> *playthings of wind and storm and chance, their*
> >   *crews*
> *gone blind, the jungle hatred*
> *crawling up on deck.*

Thou Who Walked On Galilee

"Deponent further sayeth *The Bella J*
left the Guinea Coast
with cargo of five hundred blacks and odd
for the barracoons of Florida:

"That there was hardly room 'tween-decks for half
the sweltering cattle stowed spoon-fashion there;
that some went mad of thirst and tore their flesh
and sucked the blood:

"That Crew and Captain lusted with the comeliest
of the savage girls kept naked in the cabins;
that there was one they called The Guinea Rose
and they cast lots and fought to lie with her:

"That when the Bo's'n piped all hands, the flames
spreading from starboard already were beyond
control, the negroes howling and their chains
entangled with the flames:

"That the burning blacks could not be reached,
that the Crew abandoned ship,

leaving their shrieking negresses behind,
that the Captain perished drunken with the wenches·

"Further Deponent sayeth not."

Pilot Oh Pilot Me

II.

Aye, lad, and I have seen those factories,
Gambia, Rio Pongo, Calabar;
have watched the artful mongos baiting traps
of war wherein the victor and the vanquished

Were caught as prizes for our barracoons.
Have seen the nigger kings whose vanity
and greed turned wild black hides of Fellatah,
Mandingo, Ibo, Kru to gold for us.

And there was one—King Anthracite we named him—
fetish face beneath French parasols
of brass and orange velvet, impudent mouth
whose cups were carven skulls of enemies:

He'd honor us with drum and feast and conjo
and palm-oil-glistening wenches deft in love,
and for tin crowns that shone with paste,
red calico and German-silver trinkets

Would have the drums talk war and send
his warriors to burn the sleeping villages
and kill the sick and old and lead the young
in coffles to our factories.

Twenty years a trader, twenty years,
for there was wealth aplenty to be harvested
from those black fields, and I'd be trading still
but for the fevers melting down my bones.

III.

Shuttles in the rocking loom of history,
the dark ships move, the dark ships move,
their bright ironical names
like jests of kindness on a murderer's mouth;
plough through thrashing glister toward
fata morgana's lucent melting shore,
weave toward New World littorals that are
mirage and myth and actual shore.

Voyage through death,
    voyage whose chartings are
        unlove.
A charnel stench, effluvium of living death
spreads outward from the hold,
where the living and the dead, the horribly dying,
lie interlocked, lie foul with blood and excrement.

Deep in the festering hold thy father lies,
the corpse of mercy rots with him,
rats eat love's rotten gelid eyes.

But, oh, the living look at you
with human eyes whose suffering accuses you,
whose hatred reaches through the swill of dark
to strike you like a leper's claw.

You cannot stare that hatred down
or chain the fear that stalks the watches
and breathes on you its fetid scorching breath;
cannot kill the deep immortal human wish,
the timeless will.

"But for the storm that flung up barriers
of wind and wave, *The Amistad*, señores,
would have reached the port of Príncipe in two,
three days at most; but for the storm we should
have been prepared for what befell.
Swift as the puma's leap it came. There was
that interval of moonless calm filled only
with the water's and the rigging's usual sounds,
then sudden movement, blows and snarling cries
and they had fallen on us with machete
and marlinspike. It was as though the very
air, the night itself were striking us.
Exhausted by the rigors of the storm,
we were no match for them. Our men went down
before the murderous Africans. Our loyal
Celestino ran from below with gun
and lantern and I saw, before the cane-
knife's wounding flash, Cinquez,
that surly brute who calls himself a prince,
directing, urging on the ghastly work.
He hacked the poor mulatto down, and then
he turned on me. The decks were slippery
when daylight finally came. It sickens me
to think of what I saw, of how these apes
threw overboard the butchered bodies of
our men, true Christians all, like so much jetsam.
Enough, enough. The rest is quickly told:
Cinquez was forced to spare the two of us

you see to steer the ship to Africa,
and we like phantoms doomed to rove the sea
voyaged east by day and west by night,
deceiving them, hoping for rescue,
prisoners on our own vessel, till
at length we drifted to the shores of this
your land, America, where we were freed
from our unspeakable misery. Now we
demand, good sirs, the extradition of
Cinquez and his accomplices to La
Havana. And it distresses us to know
there are so many here who seem inclined
to justify the mutiny of these blacks.
We find it paradoxical indeed
that you whose wealth, whose tree of liberty
are rooted in the labor of your slaves
should suffer the august John Quincy Adams
to speak with so much passion of the right
of chattel slaves to kill their lawful masters
and with his Roman rhetoric weave a hero's
garland for Cinquez. I tell you that
we are determined to return to Cuba
with our slaves and there see justice done.
     Cinquez—
or let us say 'the Prince'—Cinquez shall die."

The deep immortal human wish,
the timeless will:

     Cinquez its deathless primaveral image,
     life that transfigures many lives.

Voyage through death
     to life upon these shores.

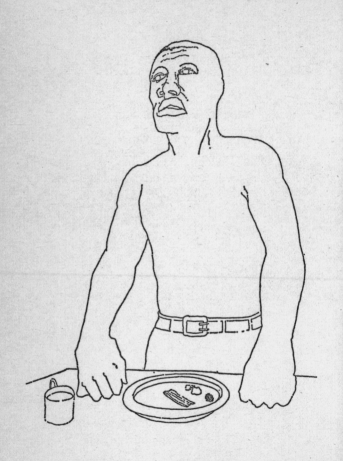

SHALL BE
REMEMBERED

Frederick Douglass

Robert Hayden

When it is finally ours, this freedom, this liberty, this
      beautiful
and terrible thing, needful to man as air,
usable as the earth; when it belongs at last to our
      children,
when it is truly instinct, brainmatter, diastole, systole,
reflex action; when it is finally won; when it is more
than the gaudy mumbo jumbo of politicians:
this man, this Douglass, this former slave, this Negro
beaten to his knees, exiled, visioning a world
where none is lonely, none hunted, alien,
this man, superb in love and logic, this man
shall be remembered—oh, not with statues' rhetoric,
not with legends and poems and wreaths of bronze
      alone,
but with the lives grown out of his life, the lives
fleshing his dream of the needful beautiful thing.

Runagate Runagate

Robert Hayden

I.

Runs falls rises stumbles on from darkness into darkness
and the darkness thicketed with shapes of terror
and the hunters pursuing and the hounds pursuing
and the night cold and the night long and the river
to cross and the jack-muh-lanterns beckoning beckoning
and blackness ahead and when shall I reach that
    somewhere
morning and keep on going and never turn back
    and keep on going.

    Runagate
            Runagate
                    Runagate

Many thousands rise and go
many thousands crossing over

                    O mythic North
             O star-shaped yonder Bible city

Some go weeping and some rejoicing
some in coffins and some in carriages
some in silks and some in shackles

Rise and go fare you well

No more auction block for me
no more driver's lash for me

    If you see my Pompey, 30 yrs of age,
    new breeches, plain stockings, negro shoes;
    if you see my Anna, likely young mulatto
    branded E on the right cheek, R on the left,
    catch them if you can and notify subscriber.
    Catch them if you can, but it won't be easy.
    They'll dart underground when you try to catch
       them,
    plunge into quicksand, whirlpools, mazes,
    turn into scorpions when you try to catch them.

And before I'll be a slave
I'll be buried in my grave

    North star and bonanza gold
    I'm bound for the freedom, freedom-bound
    and oh Susyanna don't you cry for me

               Runagate
                     Runagate

II.

Rises from their anguish and their power,

      Harriet Tubman,

      woman of earth, whipscarred,
      a summoning, a shining

Mean to be free

And this was the way of it, brethren brethren,
way we journeyed from Can't to Can.
Moon so bright and no place to hide,
the cry up and the patterollers riding,
hound dogs belling in bladed air.
And fear starts a-murbling, Never make it,
we'll never make it. *Hush that now,*
and she's turned upon us, leveled pistol
glinting in the moonlight:
Dead folks can't jaybird-talk, she says;
you keep on going now or die, she says.

Wanted Harriet Tubman alias The General
alias Moses Stealer of Slaves

In league with Garrison Alcott Emerson
Garrett Douglass Thoreau John Brown

Armed and known to be Dangerous

Wanted Reward Dead or Alive

Tell me, Ezekiel, oh tell me do you see
mailed Jehovah coming to deliver me?

Hoot-owl calling in the ghosted air,
five times calling to the hants in the air.
Shadow of a face in the scary leaves,
shadow of a voice in the talking leaves:

Come ride-a my train

Oh that train, ghost-story train
through swamp and savanna movering movering,
over trestles of dew, through caves of the wish,
Midnight Special on a saber track movering movering
first stop Mercy and the last Hallelujah.

Come ride-a my train

    Mean mean mean to be free.

Memorial Wreath

(For the more than 200,000 Negroes
who served in the Union Army
during the Civil War)

Dudley Randall

In this green month when resurrected flowers,
Like laughing children ignorant of death,
Brighten the couch of those who wake no more,
Love and remembrance blossom in our hearts
For you who bore the extreme sharp pang for us,
And bought our freedom with your lives.

                           And now,
Honoring your memory, with love we bring
These fiery roses, white-hot cotton flowers
And violets bluer than cool northern skies
You dreamed of in the burning prison fields
When liberty was only a faint north star,
Not a bright flower planted by your hands
Reaching up hardy nourished with your blood.

Fit gravefellows you are for Lincoln, Brown
And Douglass and Toussaint . . . all whose rapt eyes
Fashioned a new world in this wilderness.

American earth is richer for your bones;
Our hearts beat prouder for the blood we inherit.

Vaticide

(For Mohandas Gandhi)

MYRON O'HIGGINS

. . . he is murdered upright in the day
his flesh is opened and displayed. . . .

Into that stricken hour the hunted had gathered.
You spoke . . . some syllable of terror. *Ram!*
They saw it slip from your teeth and dangle, ablaze
Like a diamond on your mouth.
In that perilous place you fell—extinguished.
The instrument, guilt. The act was love.

Now they have taken your death to their rooms
And here in this far city a false Spring
Founders in the ruins of your quiet flesh
And deep in your marvelous wounds
The sun burns down
And the seas return to their imagined homes.

A Poem
for Black Hearts

LeRoi Jones

For Malcolm's eyes, when they broke
the face of some dumb white man. For
Malcolm's hands raised to bless us
all black and strong in his image
of ourselves, for Malcolm's words
fire darts, the victor's tireless
thrusts, words hung above the world
change as it may, he said it, and
for this he was killed, for saying,
and feeling, and being/ change, all
collected hot in his heart, For Malcolm's
heart, raising us above our filthy cities,
for his stride, and his beat, and his address
to the grey monsters of the world, For Malcolm's
pleas for your dignity, black men, for your life,
black men, for the filling of your minds
with righteousness, For all of him dead and
gone and vanished from us, and all of him which
clings to our speech black god of our time.
For all of him, and all of yourself, look up,
black man, quit stuttering and shuffling, look up,
black man, quit whining and stooping, for all of him,
For Great Malcolm a prince of the earth,
    let nothing in us rest

until we avenge ourselves for his death, stupid animals that killed him, let us never breathe a pure breath if we fail, and white men call us faggots till the end of the earth.

To Richard Wright

CONRAD KENT RIVERS

You said that your people
Never knew the full spirit of
Western Civilization.
To be born unnoticed
Is to be born black,
And left out of the grand adventure.

Miseducation, denial,
Are lost in the cruelty of oppression.
And the faint cool kiss of sensuality
Lingers on our cheeks.

The quiet terror brings on silent night.
They are driving us crazy. And our father's
Religion warps his life.

To live day by day
   Is not to live at all.

American Gothic

To Satch

SAMUEL ALLEN (PAUL VESEY)

Sometimes I feel like I will *never* stop
Just go on forever
'Til one fine mornin'
I'm gonna reach up and grab me a handfulla stars
Swing out my long lean leg
And whip three hot strikes burnin' down the heavens
And look over at God and say
How about that!

When Mahalia Sings

QUANDRA PRETTYMAN

We used to gather at the high window
of the holiness church and, on tip-toe,
look in and laugh at the dresses, too small
on the ladies, and how wretched they all
looked—an old garage for a church, for pews,
old wooden chairs. It seemed a lame excuse
for a church. Not solemn or grand,
with no real robed choir, but a loose jazz band,
or so it sounded to our mocking ears.
So we responded to their hymns with jeers.

Sometimes those holiness people would dance,
and this we knew sprang from deep ignorance
of how to rightly worship God, who after
all was pleased not by such foolish laughter
but by the stiffly still hands in our church
where we saw no one jump or shout or lurch
or weep. We laughed to hear those holiness
rhythms making a church a song fest:
we heard this music as the road to sin,
down which they traveled toward that end.

I, since then, have heard the gospel singing
of one who says I worship with clapping
hands and my whole body, God, whom we must
thank for all this richness raised from dust.

Seeing her high-thrown head reminded
me of those holiness high-spirited,
who like angels, like saints, worshiped as whole
men with rhythm, with dance, with singing soul.
Since then, I've learned of my familiar God—
He finds no worship alien or odd.

Yardbird's
Skull

(For Charlie Parker)

OWEN DODSON

The bird is lost,
Dead, with all the music:
Whole sunsets heard the brain's music
Faded to last horizon notes.
I do not know why I hold
This skull, smaller than a walnut's,
Against my ear,
Expecting to hear
The smashed fear
Of childhood from . . . bone;
Expecting to see
Wind nosing red and purple,
Strange gold and magic
On bubbled windowpanes
Of childhood. Shall I hear?
I should hear: this skull
Has been with violets
Not Yorick, or the gravedigger,
Yapping his yelling story,
This skull has been in air,
Sensed his brother, the swallow,
(Its talent for snow and crumbs).
Flown to lost Atlantis islands,
Places of dreaming, swimming, lemmings.

O I shall hear skull skull,
Hear your lame music,
Believe music rejects undertaking,
Limps back.
Remember tiny lasting, we get lonely:
Come sing, come sing, come sing sing
And sing.

IF WE
MUST DIE

If We Must Die

CLAUDE McKAY

If we must die—let it not be like hogs
Hunted and penned in an inglorious spot,
While round us bark the mad and hungry dogs,
Making their mock at our accursed lot.
If we must die—oh, let us nobly die,
So that our precious blood may not be shed
In vain; then even the monsters we defy
Shall be constrained to honor us though dead!
Oh, Kinsmen! We must meet the common foe;
Though far outnumbered, let us show us brave,
And for their thousand blows deal one deathblow!
What though before us lies the open grave?
Like men we'll face the murderous, cowardly pack,
Pressed to the wall, dying, but fighting back!

The Lynching

CLAUDE McKAY

His spirit in smoke ascended to high heaven.
His father, by the cruelest way of pain,
Had bidden him to his bosom once again;
The awful sin remained still unforgiven.
All night a bright and solitary star
(Perchance the one that ever guided him,
Yet gave him up at last to Fate's wild whim)
Hung pitifully o'er the swinging char.
Day dawned, and soon the mixed crowds came to view
The ghastly body swaying in the sun:
The women thronged to look, but never a one
Showed sorrow in her eyes of steely blue;
And little lads, lynchers that were to be,
Danced round the dreadful thing in fiendish glee.

"So Quietly"

LESLIE PINCKNEY HILL

News item from The New York Times *on the lynching of a Negro at Smithville, Ga., December 21, 1919:* "The train was boarded so quietly . . . that members of the train crew did not know that the mob had seized the Negro until informed by the prisoner's guard after the train had left the town . . . A coroner's inquest held immediately returned the verdict that West came to his death at the hands of unidentified men."

So quietly they stole upon their prey
And dragged him out to death, so without flaw
Their black design, that they to whom the law
Gave him in keeping, in the broad, bright day,
Were not aware when he was snatched away;
And when the people, with a shrinking awe,
The horror of that mangled body saw,
"By unknown hands!" was all that they could say.

So, too, my country, stealeth on apace
The soul-blight of a nation. Not with drums
Or trumpet blare is that corruption sown,
But quietly—now in the open face
Of day, now in the dark—and when it comes,
Stern truth will never write, "By hands unknown."

The Daybreakers

ARNA BONTEMPS

We are not come to wage a strife
   With swords upon this hill:
It is not wise to waste the life
   Against a stubborn will.
Yet would we die as some have done:
Beating a way for the rising sun.

Song for a Dark Girl

LANGSTON HUGHES

Way Down South in Dixie
  (Break the heart of me)
They hung my dark young lover
  To a cross roads tree.

Way Down South in Dixie
  (Bruised body high in air)
I asked the white Lord Jesus
  What was the use of prayer.

Way Down South in Dixie
  (Break the heart of me)
Love is a naked shadow
  On a gnarled and naked tree.

Old Lem

STERLING A. BROWN

I talked to old Lem
And old Lem said:
  "They weigh the cotton
  They store the corn
    We only good enough
    To work the rows;
  They run the commissary
  They keep the books
    We gotta be grateful
    For being cheated;
  Whippersnapper clerks
  Call us out of our name
    We got to say mister
    To spindling boys
  They make our figgers
  Turn somersets
  We buck in the middle
    Say, 'Thankyuh, sah.'
      They don't come by ones
      They don't come by twos
      But they come by tens.
  "Their fists stay closed
  Their eyes look straight
    Our hands stay open
    Our eyes must fall

They don't come by ones
They got the manhood
They got the courage
    They don't come by twos
  We got to slink around,
  Hangtailed hounds.
They burn us when we dogs
They burn us when we men
    They come by tens. . . .

"I had a buddy
Six foot of man
Muscled up perfect
Game to the heart
    They don't come by ones
Outworked and outfought
Any man or two men
    They don't come by twos
He spoke out of turn
At the commissary
They gave him a day
To git out the county.
He didn't take it.
He said 'Come and get me.'
They came and got him.
    And they came by tens.
He stayed in the county—
He lays there dead.

    They don't come by ones
    They don't come by twos
    But they come by tens."

Between the World and Me

RICHARD WRIGHT

And one morning while in the woods I stumbled sud-
denly upon the thing,
Stumbled upon it in a grassy clearing guarded by scaly
oaks and elms.
And the sooty details of the scene rose, thrusting themselves between the world and me. . . .

There was a design of white bones slumbering forgot-
tenly upon a cushion of ashes.
There was a charred stump of a sapling pointing a
blunt finger accusingly at the sky.
There were torn tree limbs, tiny veins of burnt leaves,
and a scorched coil of greasy hemp;
A vacant shoe, an empty tie, a ripped shirt, a lonely
hat, and a pair of trousers stiff with black blood.
And upon the trampled grass were buttons, dead
matches, butt-ends of cigars and cigarettes, peanut
shells, a drained gin-flask, and a whore's lipstick;
Scattered traces of tar, restless arrays of feathers, and
the lingering smell of gasoline.
And through the morning air the sun poured yellow
surprise into the eye sockets of a stony skull. . . .
And while I stood my mind was frozen with a cold pity
for the life that was gone.
The ground gripped my feet and my heart was circled
by icy walls of fear—

The sun died in the sky; a night wind muttered in the grass and fumbled the leaves in the trees; the woods poured forth the hungry yelping of hounds; the darkness screamed with thirsty voices; and the witnesses rose and lived:

The dry bones stirred, rattled, lifted, melting themselves into my bones.

The grey ashes formed flesh firm and black, entering into my flesh.

The gin-flask passed from mouth to mouth; cigars and cigarettes glowed, the whore smeared the lipstick red upon her lips,

And a thousand faces swirled around me, clamoring that my life be burned. . . .

And then they had me, stripped me, battering my teeth into my throat till I swallowed my own blood.

My voice was drowned in the roar of their voices, and my black wet body slipped and rolled in their hands as they bound me to the sapling.

And my skin clung to the bubbling hot tar, falling from me in limp patches.

And the down and quills of the white feathers sank into my raw flesh, and I moaned in my agony.

Then my blood was cooled mercifully, cooled by a baptism of gasoline.

And in a blaze of red I leaped to the sky as pain rose like water, boiling my limbs.

Panting, begging I clutched childlike, clutched to the hot sides of death.

Now I am dry bones and my face a stony skull staring in yellow surprise at the sun. . . .

I AM
THE DARKER
BROTHER

I, Too,
Sing America

LANGSTON HUGHES

I, too, sing America.

I am the darker brother.
They send me to eat in the kitchen
When company comes,
But I laugh,
And eat well,
And grow strong.

Tomorrow,
I'll be at the table
When company comes.
Nobody'll dare
Say to me,
"Eat in the kitchen,"
Then.

Besides,
They'll see how beautiful I am
And be ashamed—

I, too, am America.

A Black Man
Talks of Reaping

ARNA BONTEMPS

I have sown beside all waters in my day.
I planted deep, within my heart the fear
That wind or fowl would take the grain away.
I planted safe against this stark, lean year.

I scattered seed enough to plant the land
In rows from Canada to Mexico
But for my reaping only what the hand
Can hold at once is all that I can show.

Yet what I sowed and what the orchard yields
My brother's sons are gathering stalk and root,
Small wonder then my children glean in fields
They have not sown, and feed on bitter fruit.

From the Dark Tower

COUNTEE CULLEN

We shall not always plant while others reap
The golden increment of bursting fruit,
Not always countenance, abject and mute,
That lesser men should hold their brothers cheap;
Not everlastingly while others sleep
Shall we beguile their limbs with mellow flute,
Not always bend to some more subtle brute;
We were not made eternally to weep.

The night whose sable breast relieves the stark,
White stars is no less lovely being dark,
And there are buds that cannot bloom at all
In light, but crumble, piteous, and fall;
So in the dark we hide the heart that bleeds,
And wait, and tend our agonizing seeds.

On Passing Two Negroes on a Dark Country Road Somewhere in Georgia

CONRAD KENT RIVERS

This road is like a tomb
Carrying souls to stranger realms.
A broken face, patched pants, moonlight,
Late dinner and sleep in a crowded room.
Let us hope that our gods dance
And eat cornbread from a wooden spoon,
When night enters
With a cool breeze
To soothe an aching back.

Beehive

JEAN TOOMER

Within this black hive to-night
There swarm a million bees;
Bees passing in and out the moon,
Bees escaping out the moon,
Bees returning through the moon,
Silver bees intently buzzing,
Silver honey dripping from the swarm of bees
Earth is a waxen cell of the world comb,
And I, a drone,
Lying on my back,
Lipping honey,
Getting drunk with silver honey,
Wish that I might fly out past the moon
And curl forever in some far-off farmyard flower.

Tired

FENTON JOHNSON

I am tired of work; I am tired of building up somebody
    else's civilization.
Let us take a rest, M'Lissy Jane.
I will go down to the Last Chance Saloon, drink a gallon
    or two of gin, shoot a game or two of dice, and sleep
    the rest of the night on one of Mike's barrels.
You will let the old shanty go to rot, the white people's
    clothes turn to dust, and the Calvary Baptist Church
    sink to the bottomless pit.
You will spend your days forgetting you married me
    and your nights hunting the warm gin Mike serves
    the ladies in the rear of the Last Chance Saloon.
Throw the children into the river; civilization has given
    us too many. It is better to die than to grow up and
    find that you are colored.
Pluck the stars out of the heavens. The stars mark our
    destiny. The stars marked my destiny.
I am tired of civilization.

Sympathy

PAUL LAURENCE DUNBAR

I know what the caged bird feels, alas!
When the sun is bright on the upland slopes;
When the wind stirs soft through the springing grass
And the river flows like a stream of glass;
When the first bird sings and the first bud opes,
And the faint perfume from its chalice steals—
I know what the caged bird feels!

I know why he beats his wing!
Till its blood is red on the cruel bars;
For he must fly back to his perch and cling
When he fain would be on the bough a-swing;
And a pain still throbs in the old, old scars
And they pulse again with a keener sting—
I know why he beats his wing!

I know why the caged bird sings, ah me,
When his wing is bruised and his bosom sore,
When he beats his bars and would be free;
It is not a carol of joy or glee,
But a prayer that he sends from his heart's deep core,
But a plea, that upward to Heaven he flings—
I know why the caged bird sings!

Sorrow Is the
Only Faithful One

OWEN DODSON

Sorrow is the only faithful one:
The lone companion clinging like a season
To its original skin no matter what the variations.

If all the mountains paraded
Eating the valleys as they went
And the sun were a cliffure on the highest peak,

Sorrow would be there between
The sparkling and the giant laughter
Of the enemy when the clouds come down to swim.

But I am less, unmagic, black,
Sorrow clings to me more than to doomsday mountains
Or erosion scars on a palisade.

Sorrow has a song like a leech
Crying because the sand's blood is dry
And the stars reflected in the lake

Are water for all their twinkling
And bloodless for all their charm.
I have blood, and a song.
SORROW IS THE ONLY FAITHFUL ONE.

If the Stars
Should Fall

SAMUEL ALLEN (PAUL VESEY)

Again the day
The low bleak day of the stricken years
And now the years.

The huge slow grief drives on
And I wonder why
And I grow cold
And care less
And less and less I care.

If the stars should fall,
I grant them privilege;
Or if the stars should rise to a brighter flame
The mighty dog, the buckled Orion
To excellent purposes appear to gain—
I should renew their privilege
To fall down.

It is all to me the same
The same to me
I say the great Gods, all of them,
All—cold, pitiless—
Let them fall down
Let them buckle and drop.

For a Lady I Know

COUNTEE CULLEN

She even thinks that up in heaven
Her class lies late and snores,
While poor black cherubs rise at seven
To do celestial chores.

Incident

COUNTEE CULLEN

Once riding in old Baltimore,
    Heart-filled, head-filled with glee,
I saw a Baltimorean
    Keep looking straight at me.

Now I was eight and very small,
    And he was no whit bigger,
And so I smiled, but he poked out
    His tongue, and called me, "Nigger."

I saw the whole of Baltimore
    From May until December;
Of all the things that happened there
    That's all that I remember.

We Wear
the Mask

PAUL LAURENCE DUNBAR

We wear the mask that grins and lies,
It hides our cheeks and shades our eyes—
This debt we pay to human guile;
With torn and bleeding hearts we smile,
And mouth with myriad subtleties.

Why should the world be overwise,
In counting all our tears and sighs?
Nay, let them only see us, while
    We wear the mask.

We smile, but, O great Christ, our cries
To thee from tortured souls arise.
We sing, but oh the clay is vile
Beneath our feet, and long the mile;
But let the world dream otherwise,
    We wear the mask!

Hokku: In the Falling Snow

RICHARD WRIGHT

In the falling snow
A laughing boy holds out his palms
Until they are white

Yet Do I Marvel

COUNTEE CULLEN

I doubt not God is good, well-meaning, kind,
And did He stoop to quibble could tell why
The little buried mole continues blind,
Why flesh that mirrors Him must some day die,
Make plain the reason tortured Tantalus
Is baited by the fickle fruit, declare
If merely brute caprice dooms Sisyphus
To struggle up a never-ending stair.
Inscrutable His ways are, and immune
To catechism by a mind too strewn
With petty cares to slightly understand
What awful brain compels His awful hand.
Yet do I marvel at this curious thing:
To make a poet black, and bid him sing!

The Train Runs
Late to Harlem

CONRAD KENT RIVERS

Each known mile comes late.
Faces that leave with me earlier,
Return, sit and wait.
We made eight gruesome hours today.
And lunch; lunch we barely ate,
Watching today tick away.

One bravado is going to crash
One of those pine paneled suites
Where the boss sits, laying before
Him mankind's pleas. Old Boss
In his wild sophisticated way,
He'll quote from Socrates or Plato,
Then confess to be one of us.

I'll take Sunday's long way home,
Ride those waves;
Book passage around the world.
New house: boarding school for my
Kids, free rides at Riverside, buy
Out Sherman's barbecue,
Lift my people from poverty,
Until my train pops 133rd square
In her tiger's mouth
Returning me, returning me.

Award

[A gold watch to the FBI man
who has followed me for 25 years.]

RAY DUREM

Well, old spy
looks like I
led you down some pretty blind alleys,
took you on several trips to Mexico,
fishing in the high Sierras,
jazz at the Philharmonic.
You've watched me all your life,
I've clothed your wife,
put your two sons through college.
what good has it done?
sun keeps rising every morning.
Ever see me buy an Assistant President?
or close a school?
or lend money to Somoza?
I bought some after-hours whiskey in L.A.
but the Chief got his pay.
I ain't killed no Koreans,
or fourteen-year-old boys in Mississippi
neither did I bomb Guatemala,
or lend guns to shoot Algerians.
I admit I took a Negro child
to a white rest room in Texas,
but she was my daughter, only three,
and she had to pee,

and I just didn't know what to do,
would you?
see, I'm so light, it don't seem right
to go to the colored rest room;
my daughter's brown, and folks frown on that in Texas,
I just don't know how to go to the bathroom in the
    free world!

Now, old FBI man,
you've done the best you can,
you lost me a few jobs,
scared a couple landlords,
You got me struggling for that bread,
but I ain't dead.
and before it's all through,
I may be following you!

Status Symbol

MARI EVANS

    i
Have Arrived

    i
  am the
New Negro

    i
am the result of
President Lincoln
World War I
and Paris
the
Red Ball Express
white drinking fountains
sitdowns and
sit-ins
Federal Troops
Marches on Washington
   and
prayer meetings . . .

today
They hired me
it
is a status

job . . .
along
with my papers
They
gave me my
Status Symbol
the
key
to the
White . . . Locked . . .
John

Black Is a Soul

Joseph White

Down
Down into the fathomless depths
Down into the abyss beneath the stone
Down still farther, to the very bottom
    of the infinite
Where black-eyed peas & greens are stored

Where de lawd sits among melon rinds.
A dark blue sound (funky & barefooted)
    entered & sang a tear for the People
Of black women (buxom & beautiful)
With nappy heads & cocoa filled breasts
nippled with molasses,
    & their legs sensual & long beneath
    short bright dresses
& of black men greasy from the sun-soaked
    fields sitting in the shade,
    their guitars, the willow & the
    squatting sun weeping authentic blues

These quantums of pure soul
Who pick cotton under the rant rays of the sun
Who eat hot greasy fish, chitlins, corn pone,
    pig feet, fat back & drink wine
    on Sat. nights

Who get happy & swing tambourines & sing
    them there spirituals
Who are blessed by the power of poverty
Who bathe their feet in streamlets of
    simplicity
Who are torn by the insolence & depression
    of bigot blonde America,
Are the essence of beauty
The very earth
The good earth
The black earth

In these moments when my man preaches
    about a no good nigger woman who did
    him wrong
My fingers begin to pop
My feet jump alive
The blue sound clutches me to its bosom
    until I become that sound
In these moments when the sun is blue
When the rivers flow with wine
When the neck bone tree is in blossom
I raise my down bent kinky head to charlie
    & shout
I'm black. I'm black
& I'm from Look Back

THE HOPE
OF YOUR
UNBORN

The Still Voice of Harlem

CONRAD KENT RIVERS

Come to me broken dreams and all
　　bring me the glory of fruitless souls,
I shall find a place for them in my gardens.

Weep not for the golden sun of California,
　　think not of the fertile soil of Alabama . . .
nor your father's eyes, your mother's body
　　　　twisted by the washing board.

I am the hope of your unborn,
　　truly, when there is no more of me . . .
there shall be no more of you. . . .

Dream
Variation

LANGSTON HUGHES

To fling my arms wide
In some place of the sun,
To whirl and to dance
Till the white day is done.
Then rest at cool evening
Beneath a tall tree
While night comes on gently,
    Dark like me—
That is my dream!

To fling my arms wide
In the face of the sun,
Dance! Whirl! Whirl!
Till the quick day is done.
Rest at pale evening . . .
A tall, slim tree . . .
Night coming tenderly
    Black like me.

Poems for My Brother Kenneth, VII

OWEN DODSON

Sleep late with your dream.
The morning has a scar
To mark on the horizon
With death of the morning star.

The color of blood will appear
And wash the morning sky,
Aluminum birds flying with fear
Will scream to your waking,
Will send you to die;

Sleep late with your dream.
Pretend that the morning is far,
Deep in the horizon country,
Unconcerned with the morning star.

In Time
of Crisis

RAYMOND RICHARD PATTERSON

You are the brave who do not break
In the grip of the mob when the blow comes straight
To the shattered bone; when the sockets shriek;
When your arms lie twisted under your back.

Good men holding their courage slack
In their frightened pockets see how weak
The work that is done—and feel the weight
Of your blood on the ground for their spirits' sake;

And build their anger, stone on stone—
Each silently, but not alone.

The Noonday
April Sun

GEORGE LOVE

when through the winding cobbled streets of time
new spring is borne upon the voices of young boys
when all around the grass grows up like laughter
and visions grow like grass beneath our feet
then roads run out like wine
and eyes like tongues drink up the streams of longing

o then remembrance rages at the tyranny of days
and men within their shabby inward rooms
get up to press their faces to the windowpanes
and then run down in rivers to the sea of dreams

After
the Winter

CLAUDE McKAY

Some day, when trees have shed their leaves
   And against the morning's white
The shivering birds beneath the eaves
   Have sheltered for the night,
We'll turn our faces southward, love,
   Toward the summer isle
Where bamboos spire the shafted grove
   And wide-mouthed orchids smile.

And we will seek the quiet hill
   Where towers the cotton tree,
And leaps the laughing crystal rill,
   And works the droning bee.
And we will build a cottage there
   Beside an open glade,
With black-ribbed bluebells blowing near,
   And ferns that never fade.

Four Sheets to the Wind and a One-Way Ticket to France

CONRAD KENT RIVERS

As a child
I bought a red scarf and women told me
>how beautiful it looked.
Wandering through the sous-sols as France
>wandered through me.

In the evenings
I would watch the funny people make love
>the way Maupassant said.
My youth allowed me the opportunity to hear
>all those strange
verbs conjugated in erotic affirmations. I knew love at twelve.

When Selassie went before his peers and Dillinger goofed
I read in two languages, not really caring which one
>belonged to me.

My mother lit a candle for George, my father
>went broke, we died.

When I felt blue, the Champs understood, and when
>it was crowded

the alley behind Harry's New York Bar soothed
                                        my restless spirit.

I liked to watch the nonconformists gaze at the paintings
along Gauguin's bewildered paradise.

Braque once passed me in front of the Café Musique.
I used to watch those sneaky professors examine the
    populace.
Americans never quite fitted in, but they tried so we
    smiled.

I guess the money was too much for my folks.
Hitler was such a prig and a scare, we caught the long
    boat.
I stayed.

Main Street was never the same. I read Gide and tried
    to
translate Proust. Now nothing is real except French wine.
For absurdity is reality, my loneliness unreal, my mind
    tired.

And I shall die an old Parisian.

For My People

MARGARET WALKER

For my people everywhere singing their slave songs
repeatedly: their dirges and their ditties and their
blues and jubilees, praying their prayers nightly
to an unknown god, bending their knees humbly
to an unseen power;

For my people lending their strength to the years, to
the gone years and the now years and the maybe
years, washing ironing cooking scrubbing sewing
mending hoeing plowing digging planting pruning
patching dragging along never gaining never reaping never knowing and never understanding;

For my playmates in the clay and dust and sand of
Alabama backyards playing baptizing and preach-
ing and doctor and jail and soldier and school and
mama and cooking and playhouse and concert and
store and hair and Miss Choomby and company;

For the cramped bewildered years we went to school
to learn to know the reasons why and the answers
to and the people who and the places where and
the days when, in memory of the bitter hours
when we discovered we were black and poor and
small and different and nobody cared and nobody
wondered and nobody understood;

For the boys and girls who grew in spite of these things
to be man and woman, to laugh and dance and
sing and play and drink their wine and religion
and success, to marry their playmates and bear
children and then die of consumption and anemia
and lynching;

For my people thronging 47th Street in Chicago and
Lenox Avenue in New York and Rampart Street
in New Orleans, lost disinherited dispossessed and
happy people filling the cabarets and taverns and
other people's pockets needing bread and shoes
and milk and land and money and something—
something all our own;

For my people walking blindly spreading joy, losing
time being lazy, sleeping when hungry, shouting
when burdened, drinking when hopeless, tied and
shackled and tangled among ourselves by the
unseen creatures who tower over us omnisciently
and laugh;

For my people blundering and groping and floundering
in the dark of churches and schools and clubs
and societies, associations and councils and com-
mittees and conventions, distressed and disturbed
and deceived and devoured by money-hungry
glory-craving leeches, preyed on by facile force of
state and fad and novelty, by false prophet and
holy believer;

For my people standing staring trying to fashion a
better way from confusion, from hypocrisy and
misunderstanding, trying to fashion a world that

will hold all the people, all the faces, all the adams
and eves and their countless generations;

Let a new earth rise. Let another world be born. Let a
bloody peace be written in the sky. Let a second
generation full of courage issue forth; let a people
loving freedom come to growth. Let a beauty full
of healing and a strength of final clenching be the
pulsing in our spirits and our blood. Let the
martial songs be written, let the dirges disappear.
Let a race of men now rise and take control.

Notes

The Notes are listed alphabetically according to the titles of the poems and not in the order in which they appear in the text.

Award   RAY DUREM

Members of the Somoza family have controlled Nicaragua since 1936, when General Anastasio Somoza seized power.

The Assistant President referred to is Sherman Adams.

A Ballad of Remembrance   ROBERT HAYDEN

The dictionary meaning of quadroon is "one who is one-fourth Negro, the offspring of a mulatto and a white." With our modern knowledge of the inability of scientists to find exact proportions of "Negro" and "white" in a person, we know this definition is misleading. Here the word indicates racially mixed origins.

Mark Van Doren is an American poet and teacher of great renown.

Dust Bowl   ROBERT A. DAVIS

During the 1920's and through the years of the Great Depression, the rich topsoil of the once fertile lands of the Southwestern United States was blown away, leaving vast areas of dusty plain. Thousands of Americans who had settled and farmed this land were forced to migrate to usually inhospitable and poorer areas in other states.

Four Sheets to the Wind and a One-Way Ticket to France   CONRAD KENT RIVERS

The Champs Elysées is a famous boulevard on the right bank of Paris, known for its cafés, shops, and theaters.

Frederick Douglass   ROBERT HAYDEN

Frederick Douglass was born a slave. He escaped to freedom from Baltimore in 1838 and began a career as an abolitionist, writer, and orator. Working as a laborer, Douglass attended antislavery society meetings and conventions in Massachusetts, where his speeches were so eloquent that he became a lecturer for the Massachusetts Anti-Slavery Society.

Douglass escaped to England in 1845 to avoid reenslavement, but was able to return and buy his freedom. He established an abolitionist newspaper, was active as a lecturer, and supported education for the Negro and the cause of women's suffrage in this country.

He was an adviser to John Brown, and after Brown was arrested, following the 1859 raid on Harpers Ferry, Douglass had to leave America again, going first to Canada, and then to England. During the Civil War he was very active in raising regiments of Negro soldiers for the North, and he constantly agitated for civil rights and suffrage for the Negro.

His autobiography, *Life and Times of Frederick Douglass*, is a well-written and still moving account of Southern slave life, as well as the personal story of a great writer and intellect.

In 1889, his appointment as Consul-General to Haiti gave him some measure of national recognition for a life spent in service to his people and country.

His writings have provided a philosophical basis for

programs aimed at social and economic equality, both in his own time and today.

If We Must Die   CLAUDE MCKAY

When Winston Churchill, then Prime Minister of England, addressed a joint session of the United States Congress in 1941, he quoted the final lines of this poem to urge the United States to join with Europe against the German attack.

Me and the Mule   LANGSTON HUGHES

For over a century, "black" was a term used to describe Negroes as inferiors or underlings. But with the coming of a vigorous civil rights movement and the freedom from white rule of many African countries, the negative use of "black" has diminished considerably. Negro Americans began using this simple and direct word themselves with a great amount of pride, in such phrases as "I'm a black man" or "I'm a black American," and with a sense of racial identification with black peoples all over the world.

Memorial Wreath   DUDLEY RANDALL

Toussaint L'Ouverture (1743–1803) was a military and political leader and one of the liberators of Haiti.

Middle Passage   ROBERT HAYDEN

Mongo is an ethnic and linguistic division of Bantu tribes living south of the great bend of the Congo River.

Barracoons are enclosures of barracks built and used for the temporary confinement of slaves.

Conjo are African fetish objects having mystical powers, used in rituals.

Fellatah (Fellata) are Egyptian and Sudanese Negro peoples.

Ibo is one of a group of Negro tribes living on the Lower Niger River. American slaves from this region were called Eboe.

Kru is one tribe of Negro peoples from the Liberian region of Africa.

Mandingo are Negro tribes living in the Western Sudan.

The final section of this epic poem follows accounts of the *Amistad* mutiny of 1839. During their shipment as slaves in the *Amistad*, a Spanish ship, the African captives mutinied. The mutiny was successful, but the ship was steered to United States waters by one of its crew, instead of to Africa. The men were brought to New London, Connecticut, placed on trial, and defended by John Quincy Adams. The case went to the United States Supreme Court which, in a historic decision, upheld the lower court's decision, and freed the mutineers. They were allowed to return to Africa in 1841.

The Negro Speaks of Rivers   LANGSTON HUGHES

W. E. DuBois (1868–1963) was an important figure in Negro American life. He was a professor of economics, history, and sociology, and the author of many books, one of the best known of which is *The Souls of Black Folk* (1903). Mr. DuBois was a founder of the National Association for the Advancement of Colored People, and editor of its magazine, *Crisis*, in which this poem first appeared.

O Daedalus, Fly Away Home   ROBERT HAYDEN

Daedalus was a character in Greek mythology who built wings for himself and for his son, Icarus, with which they were able to fly.

Juba, a dance developed by Southern slaves, is also the name of a thousand-mile river flowing from Southern Ethiopia to the Indian Ocean.

Juju and conjo are African fetish objects having mystical powers, used in rituals.

A Poem for Black Hearts   LEROI JONES

Malcolm X was a leader in the Nation of Islam religion and shortly before his death he organized his own political and civil rights group. His assassination, while he was speaking at a meeting in New York's Audubon Ballroom, cut short his development as a leader of Afro-American thought and action.

Malcolm X was criticized severely, during his few years of activity, by both the American mass media and some Negro spokesmen. Ironically, since his death and the publication of *The Autobiography of Malcolm X*, his racial views and programs for achieving economic and political parity have been given credence by many Negro Americans. Malcolm X spoke above all else for dignity for the black man.

LeRoi Jones wrote this poem soon after Malcolm X's death in February, 1965.

Runagate Runagate   ROBERT HAYDEN

The word "runagate" is a variation on "renegade," and means a wanderer, fugitive, or runaway.

Over one hundred thousand slaves excaped from the South between 1810 and 1850, running, walking, riding along from station to station on the Underground Railroad. There were over three thousand active men and women, mostly Negro, who worked independently to help the escapees along this journey. These were the "conductors" on the "railroad," which was actually a secret network of houses, churches, inns, stores, and trails to help fugitive slaves in their flight to the North. This system is known to have existed as early as 1786, but without benefit of formal organization.

Among the thousands who guided escaping slaves to freedom was Harriet Tubman. Born about 1821, an ex-slave herself, she was known as "Moses" and "The General." She made many trips back into the Southern states, at great personal risk, to lead her family and other slaves to the North. Called "Stealer of Slaves" by the owners, she had a price on her head, and was a hunted woman who could have been shot on sight.

Until her death, Harriet Tubman was a world-renowned and eloquent voice for full freedom for the Negro American.

William Lloyd Garrison, Bronson Alcott, Ralph Waldo Emerson, Thomas Garrett, Frederick Douglass, Henry David Thoreau, and John Brown were all opposed to slavery in their writings and actions.

Status Symbol   MARI EVANS

The "Red Ball Express" was a World War II truck supply route that ran from the ports and beaches of Europe up to the front lines. Nearly all the drivers were Negro.

Tired   FENTON JOHNSON

Fenton Johnson was one of the first of the Negro American "revolutionary" poets. He broke away from the conventional approach of early twentieth-century "Negro" poetry, with its use of dialect and traditional literary form. His poems, as here shown in "Tired," are for the most part in free verse and natural speech patterns, and they echo the disillusionment Negro Americans were experiencing during the 1920's.

James Weldon Johnson wrote of Fenton Johnson's poetry in 1931: "He went further than protests against wrong or the moral challenge that the wronged can always fling against the wrongdoer; *he sounded the note of fatalistic despair.*"

Vaticide   MYRON O'HIGGINS

Mohandas Gandhi, a leader of the people of India until his assassination in 1948, fought for the independence of his nation and for various political and social programs through the use of nonviolent demonstrations, hunger fasts, and civil disobedience.

Gandhi's writings and actions have strongly influenced the Reverend Martin Luther King and other leaders of the nonviolent civil rights movement in America.

This poem was written in 1948, during the week following Gandhi's death.

Yardbird's Skull (*For Charlie Parker*)   OWEN DODSON

Charlie Parker was a jazz alto saxophone player who was an innovator in improvisation and in his approach to this truly American music. He inspired a generation of musicians and listeners. After his death there grew around his memory a legend exemplified in the slogan, "Bird Lives."

Yet Do I Marvel   COUNTEE CULLEN

Tantalus was a character in Greek mythology who was punished for revealing the secrets of the gods to men. He was condemned to an eternity of standing, hungry and thirsty, in water up to his chin, beneath a tree laden with fruit. Whenever he tried to drink or eat, the water and fruit receded.

Sisyphus was a king of Corinth, in Greek mythology, who was condemned in Hades to roll a heavy stone continually up a steep hill, only to have it roll down again each time he reached the top.

Biographies

SAMUEL ALLEN (Paul Vesey) was born in Columbus, Ohio, in 1917. He studied with James Weldon Johnson at Fisk University, received an LL.D. from Harvard Law School, and later studied at the Sorbonne, in Paris. There, Richard Wright was helpful in securing publication of Mr. Allen's poems in *Présence Africaine*, a French magazine. Using the name Paul Vesey, Mr. Allen published his first book, *El fenbeinzaehne (Ivory Tusks)*, in a bilingual edition in Germany. His poetry has since been printed in numerous magazines and anthologies in this country. He has traveled in Africa and in Latin America, and has been Assistant General Counsel in the Legal Department of the United States Information Agency. Since 1964, Mr. Allen has been working with the Community Relations Service of the Department of Justice, a Federal "civil rights" agency attempting to facilitate peaceful racial integration.

ARNA BONTEMPS was born in Alexandria, Louisiana, in 1902 and was educated at Pacific Union College and at the University of Chicago. His poetry appeared in magazines between 1924 and 1931, and won many awards and critical recognition. He has written prose books, is the author of a number of books for children, and was coeditor, with Langston Hughes, of *The Poetry of the Negro*:

1746–1949, an anthology. Mr. Bontemps has been the librarian of Fisk University since 1943.

GWENDOLYN BROOKS was born in Topeka, Kansas, and has lived in Chicago, where she received her education, almost her entire life. *A Street in Bronzeville*, published in 1945, was her first book of poems. It was followed by *Annie Allen*, which won the Pulitzer Prize for poetry in 1949. Miss Brooks is the only Negro American poet to receive that award. Other books of her poems are *The Bean Eaters* and *Selected Poems*. Miss Brooks is also the author of a novel, *Maude Martha*, and books of verse for children.

STERLING A. BROWN was born in 1901 in Washington, D.C., and was educated in that city's schools, as well as at Williams College and Harvard University. He has had a long and distinguished career at Howard University, where he holds a professorship in English and was selected to write a history of the University in 1961. His books include *Southern Road*, a volume of his poetry published in 1932; *The Negro in American Fiction* (1938), and *Negro Poetry and Drama* (1938). Mr. Brown was senior editor of the well-known anthology, *Negro Caravan*, published in 1941.

COUNTEE CULLEN was born in 1903 in New York City and was educated in the public schools of that city and at New York University. He received his master's degree from Harvard and became a teacher in New York City, a work he continued all his life. When he was twenty-two years old his first book of poems, *Color*, was published and won the Harmon Gold Award for literature. Other of his books include *Copper Sun* (1927), *The Black Christ*

(1929), *The Medea and Other Poems* (1935), and *The Lost Zoo* (1940). *On These I Stand,* published posthumously in 1947, is a volume of selected poems. Since his untimely death in 1946, Countee Cullen's reputation as a lyric poet has steadily grown.

FRANK MARSHALL DAVIS was born in Arkansas City, Kansas, in 1905. He was educated at Kansas State College and then began a career in journalism. He helped start the *Atlanta Daily World,* and later became executive editor of the *Associated Negro Press* in Chicago. He has been a Rosenwald Fellow in poetry and has published three books of his poems: *Black Man's Verse* (1935), *I Am the American Negro* (1937), and *47th Street* (1948). Mr. Davis now lives in Hawaii.

ROBERT A. DAVIS was born in Mobile, Alabama, in 1917. He attended high school in Chicago, and the University of Chicago and Chicago Christian Junior College. He has contributed to magazines, and has been active in theater productions in the Chicago area.

OWEN DODSON was born in 1914 in Brooklyn, New York, and was educated in the public schools of that borough and at Bates College. He received a Master of Fine Arts degree at Yale, where two of his plays were produced. Other plays have been produced at various colleges. Mr. Dodson is head of the Department of Drama at Howard University, in Washington, D.C. *Powerful Long Ladder,* a collection of his poems, was published in 1946.

PAUL LAURENCE DUNBAR was born in Dayton, Ohio, in 1872, the son of former slaves (his father had escaped by way of the Underground Railroad). He was unable to attend college and went to work as an elevator operator. He was holding this job when his first volume of poems, *Oak and Ivy*, appeared in 1893. *Majors and Minors* followed in 1895. They paved the way for the great success of Dunbar's *Lyrics of a Lowly Life*, published in 1896. This book gave Dunbar a national reputation, the first time in 125 years (since Phillis Wheatley) that a Negro American poet had received such wide recognition. Dunbar continued to write much poetry and prose, even though suffering from tuberculosis, which finally caused his early death, in 1906. His *Complete Poems* was published in 1913 and heralded the new era in literature that began in the early twentieth century for the Negro American.

RAY DUREM was born in Seattle, Washington, in 1915. He joined the Navy at fourteen and later fought as a member of the International Brigades during the Spanish Civil War. He lived for many years in Mexico, and returned to the United States for medical treatment. He died in Los Angeles, California, in December, 1963, prior to the publication of many of his poems. His work has appeared in the magazines *Umbra* and *Negro Digest* as well as in many anthologies both here and in Europe.

MARI EVANS was born and educated in Toledo, Ohio, and now makes her home in Indianapolis, Indiana, where she edits an industrial magazine. She has been a songwriter, civil service employee, and choir director, and she plays both piano and organ. She publishes in numerous magazines and is active at writers' conferences.

ROBERT HAYDEN was born in 1913 in Detroit, attended Wayne State University in that city, then held a teaching assistantship at the University of Michigan. He has received Hopwood awards for poetry on two occasions, and he has won fellowships from the Rosenwald and Ford foundations. He has published *Heartshape in the Dust; The Lion and the Archer*, a joint publication with Myron O'Higgins of their poetry; and *A Ballad of Remembrance. A Ballad of Remembrance* won first prize at the International Festival of Negro Arts held in 1966 at Dakar, Senegal. His *Selected Poems* was published in 1966. His poetry has appeared in *The Atlantic Monthly, Poetry, Negro Digest,* and other publications and anthologies. He joined the faculty of Fisk University in 1946 and is an associate professor of English.

CALVIN C. HERNTON was born in Chattanooga, Tennessee, in 1932, and studied at Talladega College and Fisk University in Alabama. He has taught at Edward Waters College in Jacksonville and at other Southern colleges. A writer of fiction and plays as well as poetry, Mr. Hernton has also been an editor of *Umbra* magazine. He lives in New York City.

LESLIE PINCKNEY HILL was born in 1880 in Lynchburg, Virginia, where he was educated. He attended Harvard University, taught at Tuskegee Institute, and later became the principal of the Cheyney Training School for Teachers in Pennsylvania. His published works include *The Wings of Oppression* and *Toussaint L'Ouverture—A Dramatic History.* Mr. Hill died in 1960.

LANGSTON HUGHES was born in Joplin, Missouri, in 1902, and went to school in Lawrence, Kansas, and

Cleveland, Ohio. He attended Columbia University, worked at odd jobs, shipped on freighters to Africa and to Europe, and returned to study at Lincoln University in Pennsylvania, from which he graduated in 1929. He received many awards and honors, crossed the country on numerous occasions to give public readings of his poetry, and was a prolific writer for over forty years. He wrote novels, books of short stories, plays, newspaper columns, books for children, history books, and volumes of poetry, beginning with *The Weary Blues*, in 1926. His *Selected Poems* and *The Langston Hughes Reader* both appeared in 1958. Mr. Hughes made his home in New York City and was active in helping young writers who sought his advice and personal warmth. *Panther and the Lash*, a collection of his poetry, was published soon after his death in 1967.

FENTON JOHNSON was born in 1888 in Chicago, and educated in that city. He attended the University of Chicago and produced original plays at the old Pekin Theatre on South State Street. He also edited and published several "little" literary magazines. *A Little Dreaming*, published in 1914, was his first volume of poetry. It was followed by *Visions of the Dusk* and *Songs of the Soil*. He published a book of short stories, *Tales of Darkest America*, in 1920. Mr. Johnson died in 1958.

JAMES WELDON JOHNSON was born in 1871 in Jacksonville, Florida, was educated in that city, and then attended Atlanta University. He had distinguished careers as public school principal, lawyer, diplomat, executive secretary of the N.A.A.C.P., and professor of literature at Fisk University. He and his brother were the authors of "Lift Every

Voice and Sing," a song that has become an unofficial anthem for the Negro people in the United States. Johnson also wrote lyrics for musical shows and song hits. Among his many published works are: *Fifty Years and Other Poems* (1917); *God's Trombones* (1927); *St. Peter Relates an Incident* (1930); and his autobiography, *Along This Way* (1933). He edited *The Book of American Negro Poetry*, first issued in 1922. Mr. Johnson died in an automobile accident in 1938.

LEROI JONES was born in Newark, New Jersey, in 1934. He studied at Howard and Columbia universities and at the New School in New York City. He has been an editor of *Yugen* and *Kulchur* magazines, and has published his poetry extensively in many others, as well as being a writer on jazz for *Downbeat, Metronome,* and other publications. *Preface to a Twenty Volume Suicide Note* was his first book of poems, published in 1961. He is also the author of *The Dead Lecturer* (1964), a book of poems, and several plays which have been produced with much success in New York City. *Dutchman,* one of his plays, has been made into a motion picture.

GEORGE LOVE was born in Charlotte, North Carolina. He graduated from Morehouse College in Atlanta, has worked for the United States Government in Indonesia, and has traveled widely in South America and Europe. His poems have been published in *New Negro Poets,* a collection edited by Langston Hughes. Mr. Love is also an art photographer and has exhibited his work in a New York gallery.

CLAUDE MCKAY was born in Jamaica, the British West Indies, in 1891, but came to America in his early twenties to study at Tuskegee Institute in Alabama, and then at Kansas State University. He was involved in the literary life in New York City during the 1920's and was an associate editor of the *Liberator* under Max Eastman. *Harlem Shadows*, a book of poems published in 1922, was widely acclaimed. McKay spent almost ten years living abroad and published much prose, including *Home to Harlem* (1928), *Banjo* (1929), and *A Long Way from Home* (1937). He died in 1948. His *Selected Poems* was published posthumously in 1953.

MYRON O'HIGGINS was born in Chicago in 1918. He was a student of Sterling A. Brown at Howard University, received Julius Rosenberg and Lucy Moten fellowships, and has studied and traveled widely abroad. His poems have been published in *The Lion and the Archer*, a collection he and Robert Hayden issued privately in 1948, and in many magazines and anthologies. In recent years, he received a graduate degree at Yale, has been on the staff of the Museum of Primitive Art in New York City, and has been writing experimental plays.

RAYMOND RICHARD PATTERSON was born in 1929 in New York City. He received his education at Lincoln University in Pennsylvania and at New York University. His poems have appeared in two British anthologies, *Sixes and Sevens* and *Beyond the Blues*, as well as in collections and magazines in this country. He is the author of short stories and a novel and teaches English in the New York City public schools. Mr. Patterson is a participant in the

New York State Council on the Arts poetry reading project and gives readings throughout the state.

QUANDRA PRETTYMAN was born in Baltimore, Maryland. She graduated from Antioch College and held a teaching fellowship at the University of Michigan, where she did graduate work. Miss Prettyman has been a lecturer at the New School and a faculty member of the New York College of Insurance and the Summer Program at Connecticut College. She is married and lives in New York City.

DUDLEY RANDALL was born in Washington, D.C., in 1914. He graduated from Wayne University in Detroit, received his master's degree in library science from the University of Michigan, and has been librarian of Lincoln University in Missouri and of Morgan College in Baltimore. He makes his home in Detroit and is associated with the Wayne County Public Library. Mr. Randall's poetry has appeared in *Midwest Journal, Umbra,* and *Free Lance,* as well as in many anthologies. He published *Poem Counterpoem,* in collaboration with Margaret Danner. Mr. Randall also runs the Broadside Press in Detroit, a company devoted to the publication of poetry by Negro American poets.

CONRAD KENT RIVERS was born in Atlantic City, New Jersey, in 1933. He graduated from Wilberforce University and did graduate work at Indiana University and the Chicago Teacher's College. He was published in the *Kenyon Review, Antioch Review,* and *Negro Digest,* as well as in other magazines and in anthologies. A booklet of poems, *Perchance to Dream, Othello,* appeared in 1959. *These Black*

Bodies and This Sunburnt Face was published in 1962. Mr. Rivers, who lived and taught in Chicago, died in 1967.

JEAN TOOMER was born in Washington, D.C., in 1894 and was educated at the University of Wisconsin and the College of the City of New York. His poems, short stories, and plays were published in the 1920's and received much praise from Sherwood Anderson, Hart Crane, and others. His work was collected in *Cane*, published in 1923. He died in 1967.

MARGARET WALKER was born in Birmingham, Alabama. She received a Master of Arts degree from the University of Iowa and has been on the faculty of Jackson State College in Jackson, Mississippi, for many years. Her first book of poems, *For My People*, won the Yale University Younger Poets competition and was published in 1942. She has also received a Rosenwald fellowship and has been a visiting lecturer at several colleges. Her first novel, *Jubilee* (1966), won a Houghton-Mifflin Literary Fellowship.

JOSEPH WHITE was born in Philadelphia but resides in New York City when he is not pursuing his travels and study. He has been published in the magazine *Dasein*, in *Burning Spear* (1963), a collection of poetry by Negro Americans, and in *Poets of Today*, an anthology of modern poetry.

RICHARD WRIGHT was born on a plantation near Natchez, Mississippi, in 1908. He was, for the most part, self-educated, and worked at many jobs until the publication of his first book, *Uncle Tom's Children*, in 1938. He received a Guggenheim Fellowship and published his first novel, *Native Son*, in 1940. It was a national sensation, and this success was followed five years later with an autobiography, *Black Boy*. Wright continued to publish while living in New York City, but then moved with his family to France and remained an expatriate until his death in 1960.

INDEX

INDEX TO AUTHORS

133

INDEX TO FIRST LINES